MORTIMER K. SAVES THE DAY

by Rita Golden Gelman

illustrated by Bernie Gruver

SCHOLASTIC BOOK SERVICES

NEW YORK · TORONTO · LONDON · AUCKLAND · SYDNEY · TOKYO

ISBN 0-590-30564-6

12 11 10 9 8 7 6 5 4 3 2 1   1   2 3 4 5 6/8

Printed in the U.S.A.

09

Dedicated to Trina and Teri
who cast him in his first role

"How do you do, Sir.

I'm Mortimer K.

I can sing.

I can act.

I can do the ballet.

Do you have a part for me

in your play?"

"No, I do not, Mr. Mortimer K.
You are not what I need.
Please, go away."

"Oh, Sir, you are wrong.

I am just what you need.

I can laugh.

I can cry.

I can write.

I can read."

You are not what I need. Mr. Mortimer K.

"Oh, no, you are not,

Please, go away."

"Give me a chance.

Just look at me dance.

Look at my leap

and my twirl."

"You are not what I need, Mr. Mortimer K.

What I need for my play

is a girl."

"A girl," thought Mortimer K.

to himself.

"Hmmmmm, that's a very good part."

"A skirt,
a wig,
some gloves,
a hat.

Oh, Mortimer, you're so smart."

"Hello, hello, hello, hello.
I've come to star in your
musical show.

I sing.

I dance.

I'm really a pro.

I'm sure you need me."

"The answer is NO!

What I need is a goat to star in my play.

You are not what I need.

Please, go away."

"A goat is easy," thought Mortimer K.

"Just a couple of horns and a beard."

"Sir, I'm a goat.

Will you give me a part?"

"You're a terrible goat," the man sneered.

You are not what I need.

Go away. You're not right.

What I need is a rabbit dressed up

as a knight."

"A rabbit. A rabbit.

I'll paint myself white.

I'll put on some ears.

And I'll dress like a knight.

I'll carry a carrot.

I'll puff up my tail.

"What a fine looking rabbit.

This time I won't fail."

"I am here for the part.

I am ready to start.

What do you want me to do?"

"Not a thing! You're too late.

This rabbit is great.

And I certainly cannot have two.

You are not what I need.

I am sure you'll agree.

I'll be all finished up

once I locate a bee."

"A couple of feelers.

A couple of wings.

A couple of stripes.

And a few furry things.

"Hi there, Sir. Hi!

I was just walking by,

And I said to myself, 'Oh gee.

What a wonderful day to be in a play.'

Do you have a part for a bee?"

"I do.

Yes, I do.

But I do not need you.

Go away.

Go away.

Go away.

You are not what I need, Mr. Mortimer K.

You are not what I need in my play."

So Mortimer sat in his wings and his hat.

He was sad. He was mad at the man.

He wanted so badly to be in that play.

But that play . . .

it never began.

For just as the play was about to begin,

the bee stung the goat, who started to spin.

He butted the girl right onto a mat.

        And when she rolled over,

        the rabbit was flat.

The ambulance came and took them away.

And that's when the man said to Mortimer K.,

"My actors are gone.

They have ruined my play."

"Don't worry.

I'll help you," said Mortimer K.

Then Mortimer danced in his

wings and his hat.

He buzzed like a bee.

And he did more than that . . . .

He put on his skirt and his gloves

and his hair.

And he wiggled his toes

while he jumped in the air.

Then he sang twenty songs

with his ears on his head.

"That rabbit is great,"

the audience said.

Then he put on his horns.

And he glued on his beard.

And he twirled and he leaped while

the audience cheered.

"More, we want more,"

the audience pleaded.

And the little man said,

"YOU ARE JUST WHAT I NEEDED!"